10305939

Beauty
and the
Booster

The Story of Esther

Written and Illustrated by
Damon J. Taylor

KREGEL
Kidzone

FOR PARENTS
with Dr. Sock

This story will help children learn about bravery. It comes from the Old Testament book of Esther. Esther may not have been a typical hero, but she showed great bravery and became a hero to her people.

> HERE ARE ZUM FUN ACTIVITIES FOR ZOO PARENTS TO DO VISS ZEE LITTLE KIDDIES.

Read It Together–

The story of Esther is an entire book of the Old Testament, but at only ten chapters in length, you can read it together in a few minutes.

Sharing–

Share about a time when you were afraid of something. Your kids may think you have never known fear! Let them know that it's all right to be afraid and that God takes care of His people.

Discussion Starters–

• When was the last time you were afraid?
• Why do you think Esther hid the fact that she was Jewish?
• How did God work to help His people?
• What are some ways you can demonstrate bravery?

For Fun–

What laws would you pass if you were a king or queen? What would you call your country?

Draw–

Make a flag for your imaginary country. Draw your dream castle. Create a picture of what you think Esther's garden may have looked like.

Prayer Time–

Thank God for taking care of you, and ask Him to help you to be brave.

COLEMAN HAS FOUND THAT THE LIFE OF A LITTLE BOY

can be tough at times, especially if that boy has a baby sister named Shelby. When Shelby was born, Coleman needed a way to deal with his day-to-day problems. He found his socks. Yes, that's right, his socks.

It may seem weird, but these aren't your regular, everyday tube socks that you find in your dresser. As ordinary as they may appear, these socks really are Coleman's friends, and they help him with his problems. When life gets complicated, Coleman goes to his bedroom and works through his troubles by playing make-believe with his socks and remembering Bible stories he's learned.

So please sit back, take off your shoes and socks if you like, and enjoy Coleman's imaginary world in . . .

Beauty
and the
Booster
The Story of Esther

It was the dreaded "B" day on the calendar at home—"Booster Day." Coleman and Shelby were due to receive their shots at the doctor's office. Coleman hated getting shots, and he was nervous about going to see the doctor.

And Shelby? Well, that's another story. She lived in fear of going to the doctor's office. To get her into the car, her mom and dad told her they were going to get ice cream. After the shots, they *would* go for ice cream.

The last time Shelby went to the doctor's office for her shots, it took five people to hold her down.

While they were waiting, Coleman's dad said, "Coleman, you're Shelby's big brother, and you should get your shot first. Shelby will see your good example, and won't have as much trouble as she did the last time."

"I hate shots just as much as Shelby does," thought Coleman. "Why should I have to go first? It's not fair! Shelby is being a baby. All girls are scaredy-cat babies!"

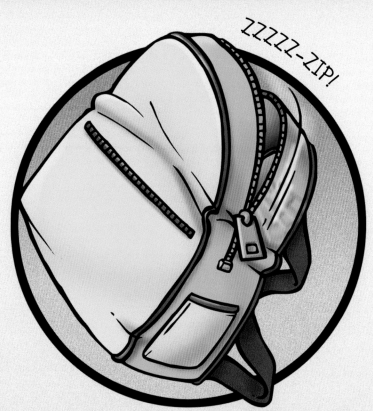

ZZZZZ-ZIP!

"Hey, where are you going?" came a muffled voice from Coleman's backpack. "*I* tell the stories! You just act them out."

"Not this time, buddy. Coleman has gone too far. I'll show him who's a scaredy-cat baby!" came another voice.

There seemed to be an argument going on in Coleman's backpack. Coleman thought he heard Sockariah, his sock friend.

"Hi, Sockariah . . . wait, you're not Sockariah!" said Coleman.

"Nope, I'm Sockette," said the pink girl's sock as she and Sockariah worked their way out of Coleman's backpack.

"How did a girl's sock get into my backpack? SHELBY!" hollered Coleman.

"Did I hear you say that *all* girls are scaredy-cat babies? Don't you remember the story of Esther?"

"Who's Esther?" asked Coleman.

CAN I AT LEAST BE UNCLE MORDECAI?

"You just sit back and let me tell you about Esther," said Sockette.

Esther was the prettiest girl in the land of Persia. Everywhere she went, men noticed her beauty. One day, she caught the attention of someone really special.

"Wow, would you look at her!" said Xerxes, the king of Persia. "She has to be the prettiest girl I've ever seen. I want her to be my queen."

Xerxes was a powerful king, and what he wanted, he always got. Esther became his queen.

Esther wasn't only beautiful on the outside, she was even lovelier on the inside. Her heart was fully devoted to God. Xerxes was won over by Esther's beauty. He didn't know much about her or her faith, he just knew he loved her.

Just a short while ago, Esther was a poor Jewish girl. Now look at her! As the queen of Persia, Esther was given whatever she desired.

One day Esther's uncle Mordecai, a man of great faith, came to visit her at the palace.

"It is an honor for our people to have someone so close to the king," said Mordecai to his niece.

"The king doesn't know I'm Jewish," Esther said, "and I'm afraid that if he finds out, I might lose favor with him."

"Let's just keep it a secret for right now," said Uncle Mordecai.

"See?"said Coleman. "*All* girls are scaredy-cat babies."

That very same day, on his way out of the castle, Mordecai heard two of the palace guards talking about killing the king.

"Tonight, when all are asleep, we will sneak into the king's bedroom and kill him," said one man to the other.

Mordecai hurried back to Esther and told her what

he had overheard. Esther informed the king, and he had the two bad men arrested. King Xerxes was so thankful to Mordecai that he had Mordecai's name put into the king's book of favors.

"A favor from the king may come in handy someday," thought Mordecai.

At about this same time, another man was finding favor in the eyes of Xerxes. This man was Haman. He was an evil man who wanted power. He moved up the ranks in the Persian government until he became prime minister. Haman had found his place in life. King Xerxes promised Haman that all of Persia would bow down before him as he passed by. Haman liked that part best of all.

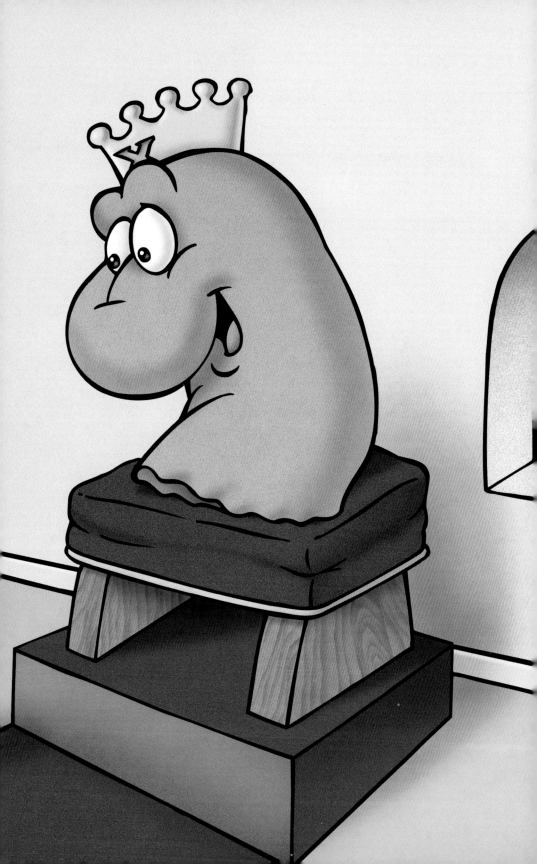

One day, as Haman was passing through the city, he came upon Esther's uncle Mordecai.

"Bow before me!" he commanded Mordecai.

"I will not," replied Mordecai. "I will only bow to honor my God, not man."

Haman was so mad, he almost blew his top!

"How dare lowly Mordecai refuse to give me honor! How dare he not bow to me as the king ordered?!" thought Haman as he threw a temper tantrum. "I will get even with this Mordecai," thought Haman. "Better yet, I will get even with all of his kind." Haman began right then to make plans to get rid of all the Jews in Persia.

Haman met with the king and said, "Some citizens are refusing to obey your commands. They do not recognize you as their leader. I think it would be wise to destroy them all before they try to hurt you."

Xerxes took Haman's advice and put Haman in charge of the plan. Haman was pleased with how his plan to get back at Mordecai was going. He had a gallows built just for Mordecai.

"What's a *gallows?*" asked Coleman.
"A gallows is a wooden structure made for hanging people from a rope to kill them," said Sockette. "Evil Haman wanted to see Mordecai die for not bowing down to him."

THIS FOOL BELIEVES EVERYTHING I TELL HIM.

News of the plan got back to Mordecai. He felt very sad for himself and his people. As was the custom for the Jews, Mordecai tore his clothes and threw ashes on himself to show how sad he was. Esther heard about her uncle's unhappiness and wanted to know what was wrong.

"Uncle, why are you so sad?" asked Esther.

"Haven't you heard? Your husband, the king, has ordered that all Jews be put to death!" cried Mordecai. "You must go to him and make him change his mind. Surely God has put you in this position so that you can save your people."

Esther was frightened. She knew that it would be almost impossible to convince her husband to change his mind. She was afraid to reveal her true faith to Xerxes, but she asked Mordecai to pray for her. She would do whatever God required of her.

"Does that sound like something a scaredy-cat baby would do?" asked Sockette.

Esther went to the king and pled for her life and for the lives of the Jews.

A GIRL'S GOTTA DO WHAT A GIRL'S GOTTA DO!

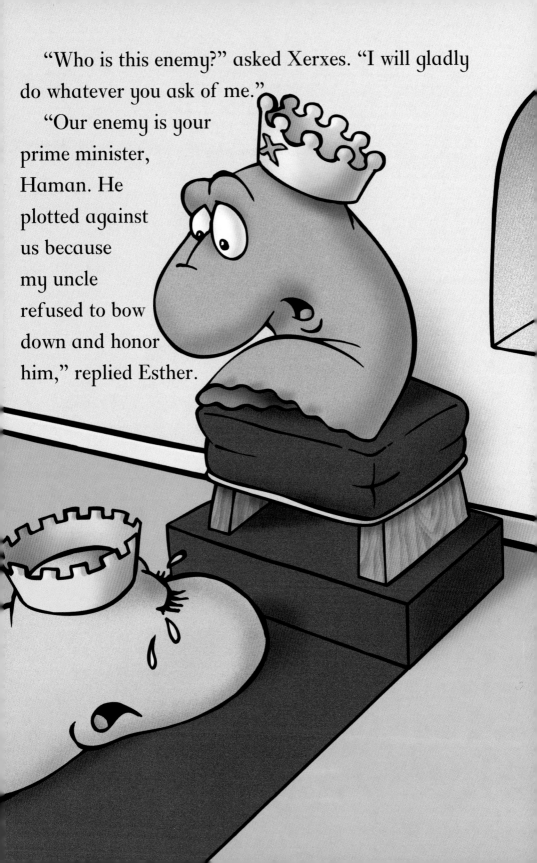

"Who is this enemy?" asked Xerxes. "I will gladly do whatever you ask of me."

"Our enemy is your prime minister, Haman. He plotted against us because my uncle refused to bow down and honor him," replied Esther.

Xerxes had Haman brought before him and sentenced him to hang from the same gallows Haman had built for Mordecai.

Xerxes needed someone to help him rule Persia, so Xerxes gave Mordecai Haman's job of prime minister. Mordecai was very proud of Esther. She had risked her life and position as queen to save her people.

"So, Coleman, did you learn anything from this story?" asked Sockette.

"Sure. I learned that I'd like to be a king when I grow up and that we can always trust God to help us be brave. Even a scaredy-cat baby like Shelby . . . hey, where *is* Shelby?"

"While you and Sockette were playing make believe, the doctor called her in for her shot," said Sockariah.

"She went on her own? Without fighting or biting? Boy, she is braver than I thought," said Coleman.

"Coleman, you're next," said the nurse.

"Next?! It's m-my turn n-now? . . . NOOOOOOO!"

The Child Sockology Series